TERROR at the GHOST TOWN MINE

by Michael Teitelbaum

illustrated by Olga and Aleksey Ivanov

BEARPORT
PUBLISHING

New York, New York

Credits

Cover: © Darryl MONTREUIL/Shutterstock, © Oleksii Zelivianskyi/Shutterstock, and © Gert Hochmuth/Shutterstock.

Publisher: Kenn Goin
Creative Director: Spencer Brinker
Text produced by Scout Books & Media Inc.

Library of Congress Cataloging-in-Publication Data in process at time of publication (2016)
Library of Congress Control Number: 2015019977
ISBN-13: 978-1-62724-811-2

For more information, write to Bearport Publishing Company, Inc., 45 West 21st Street, Suite 3B, New York, New York 10010. Printed in the United States of America.

10 9 8 7 6 5 4 3 2

Contents

CHAPTER 1

Way Out West

Twelve-year-old Jacob Lockley and his eleven-year-old brother, Rich, stared out the window from the backseat of their parents' car. The Lockley family was taking a road trip through the old mining country of California for their vacation.

"I can't believe miners found gold here," said Rich. "It looks like there's nothing but a desert."

"Look out there," said Rich's dad, pointing out the car's front window.

Rich looked ahead, his blonde hair blowing in the breeze from the car's open window. He saw rolling hills and tall mountains rising from the **barren** land.

"The gold was found in the rivers and in mines, deep inside those mountains," Dad explained. "When the gold was discovered in the 1800s, a lot of people came here looking to

get rich. That time was called the Gold Rush. Our first stop is the Miner's Museum, just up the road."

"It would be cool to see a real gold mine," said Jacob. "But only if we can take home any gold we find."

"There probably isn't any gold left in the mountains," said their mom.

"But at least you can see what life was like back then at the museum," said their dad just as they pulled into the parking lot.

The front door of the museum was designed to look like the entrance to a gold mine. An arch of fake rocks surrounded the door, and railroad tracks like the ones used in mines led up to the entrance.

"Cool!" said Rich as the family entered the museum.

During the museum tour, Jacob and Rich learned about the Gold Rush. They saw the tools that miners used, including picks, axes, shovels, and special pans for **sifting** gold out of rivers and streams. The brothers even sat in a real mining handcart, the kind that rolled on tracks deep into the mountains.

"Wow, gold! These are amazing," Jacob said, eyeing some gold nuggets.

"Ah, but they're not real," said a museum guard standing nearby. "They're just painted rocks."

"I wish I could see what it was like when miners were here in the 1800s," Rich said.

"Well, you can," said the museum guard.

"What do you mean?" asked the boys' mom.

"Not far from here is an old mining town called Hardstone," the guard explained. "It still looks exactly as it did during the Gold Rush. It's a ghost town, all right. It's as close as you'll get to going back in time."

"It sounds fascinating," Dad remarked.

"Can we go?" Jacob asked his folks.

"Please?" pleaded Rich. "Please?"

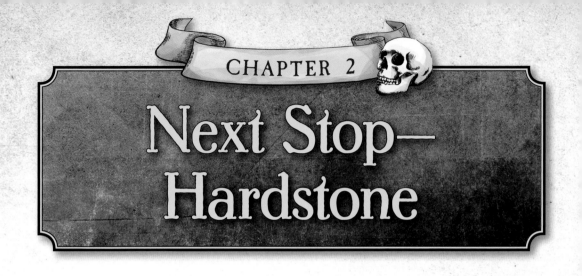

CHAPTER 2

Next Stop— Hardstone

"I'm not really interested in seeing a ghost town," said Mom. "I'd like to go to the Golden State Bookstore, which is just a couple minutes away. But you boys seem so excited about the ghost town . . ."

"Here's what we'll do," Dad exclaimed. "*I'll* go with the boys. You can drop us off. That way you can visit the bookstore while we explore the ghost town."

Mom quickly agreed, and after a short ride, the family arrived at the town of Hardstone. Getting out of the car, they all gathered around a sign that told about the town's history.

The town of Hardstone was founded in 1849, at the beginning of the Gold Rush. The town and its population peaked during the 1850s. However, when the Gold Rush ended, the town was quickly **abandoned**. It has remained a ghost town since then.

"Do you think there are any ghosts in this ghost town?" Rich asked nervously.

"It's just an expression, honey," said his mom. "Just a term used to describe a town where no one lives anymore."

That made Rich feel better.

"I'll meet you right back here in an hour," said Mom. "Have fun, guys!"

Dad, Jacob, and Rich watched her drive off, then they turned and headed into Hardstone.

The two brothers walked down Hardstone's Main Street. Dad **trudged** behind. Suddenly, they heard footsteps following them.

Jacob spun around. "Hello?"

No one was there.

"It's just the wind, boys," their dad mumbled while yawning.

They stepped up onto the porch of a run-down building, and their dad plopped into an old rocking chair. His eyes started to droop and, within minutes, he was sound asleep and snoring. Jacob whispered to Rich, "Shhh . . . Let's let him sleep." The two boys quietly snuck off.

The brothers had only taken a few steps down the street when the sound of a faint voice caused Rich to freeze. "Did you hear that?" he asked.

"Wh-who's there?" Jacob stammered.

"Get out!" the voice said, a little louder this time.

Jacob and Rich looked around. They saw no one.

"It must have been the wind," said Jacob as the two came to an old general store. "Come on. Let's go in here."

Inside the store, Jacob looked
at the floor-to-ceiling shelves. He
saw canned foods, **bolts** of fabric,
and mining supplies.

Rich grabbed a pan used
for sifting gold from wet sand
and stones. Suddenly, the pan
started glowing red-hot. Rich
cried out in pain, dropping the
pan onto the floor.

"What happened?" asked Jacob.

"I don't know," said Rich. "The
pan got really hot. I burned my finger."

Jacob looked at his brother's hand and
saw a small red burn mark on his thumb.

"But how could that have—"

Jacob was cut short by an axe that dropped from a high
shelf. "Look out!" he cried, pushing Rich out of the way. The
sharp tool slammed into the wooden floor, right where Rich
had been standing.

"Let's get out of here!" shouted Rich.

Outside, they heard the voice again.

"Get out!" it cried in a **strained** tone, just barely noticeable over the wind.

Rich started running. Jacob chased after him.

"Maybe Mom was wrong," said Rich, looking back over his shoulder. "Maybe there really are ghosts in this ghost town!"

Before Jacob could say anything, a huge gust of wind whipped up a small tornado of gray sand—a dust devil! The swirling sand moved toward the boys.

"We have to get indoors!" shouted Jacob.

The boys ducked into the nearest building, bursting through swinging half-doors.

As Jacob caught his breath, he saw they were inside an old saloon. A huge bar took up one side of the room. The wall behind the bar was covered in big mirrors and had shelves lined with old dusty bottles and glasses. The room was filled with wooden tables and chairs.

Before the boys had a chance to talk about what had just happened, a piano started playing—all by itself.

Rich screeched, startled by the sudden sound of music.

"Relax, Rich," said Jacob. "It must be a player piano. They have paper rolls of music that make the keys move by themselves. I'll show you."

The boys walked over to the piano. Jacob examined it closely but found no paper rolls. "This is just a regular piano!" he said in shock as the keys kept playing by themselves.

The piano playing stopped suddenly. Jacob sat down on the dusty old piano bench. He reached toward the keys to play a few notes.

But before he could touch a single key, Jacob felt an unseen force shove him off the bench. He landed on the floor, then scrambled to his feet just as a large glass bottle sailed off a shelf and zoomed past his head.

The bottle smashed against a wall, sending **shards** of glass everywhere.

"What's going on?" shouted Rich, feeling more and more uneasy.

Before Jacob could answer, a table flipped over, then a chair rose into the air and crashed onto the floor. Tables, chairs, glasses, and bottles flew through the air, going in every direction.

"This looks like that movie we watched with Dad!" cried Rich, ducking to avoid a flying chair.

"The Western movie with the big bar fight?" asked Jacob, leaning back as a bottle sailed past his face.

"Yeah, except for one thing," said Rich, inching toward the door. "There aren't any people here!"

"Let's go!" shouted Jacob.

"I'm right behind you!" Rich yelled.

The two boys raced for the door, keeping low to avoid getting hit by any flying objects.

They burst through the swinging saloon doors and ran down the street, with no idea where they were headed.

Without looking back, the boys ran until they were well past the rest of the buildings down Main Street. When they finally slowed to a stop, they found themselves just outside of town.

"Do you think those ghosts in the saloon will come after us?" asked Rich.

"Come on," said Jacob. "You know there's no such thing as ghosts. I bet the whole thing is **rigged** somehow to scare tourists like us."

A sudden gust of wind blew away a **tumbleweed**, revealing a faded wooden sign that said MINE with an arrow pointing to a path.

"The gold mine!" cried Jacob. "We've got to go see that!"

The brothers followed the path and came to a hill with a doorway built into it. The boys peered in cautiously. There was a wooden frame around an opening in the side of the hill. They could see a tunnel with railroad tracks going deep inside the hill. This was the entrance to the old mine.

"Should we go in?" asked Rich anxiously as the two boys leaned into the dark entrance. "You know Dad would never let us."

Before Jacob could answer, a blast of **frigid** air struck their faces. Sounds of metal clanging and water rushing came from inside the mine.

"Something's going on in there," said Jacob.

Then the unmistakable sound of human voices poured from the mine.

"There are people in there!" shouted Rich.

Jacob spotted an old handcart sitting on the tracks leading down into the mine. "Come on!" he said, jumping into the cart.

"I don't know," said Rich.

"You wanted to see an old mine," said Jacob. "Here's your chance! You might even see some gold in there!"

Rich **reluctantly** climbed into the handcart. He and his brother each held on to a handle and started pumping to make the cart move. The cart rolled along the tracks and into the mine.

Racing downhill through the darkness, the cart picked up speed. The boys were surprised to see oil lamps flickering along the wall. Luckily, the lamps gave off just enough light for Jacob to see that the tracks curved sharply to the right, causing two of the cart's wheels to lift off the track.

"Hang on!" shouted Jacob, leaning his weight to the left.

A low overhead wooden beam came into view. Jacob realized that Rich had his back to it.

"Duck!" Jacob shouted, just in time for both boys to squat down and narrowly pass under the thick beam.

The cart slowed as it neared the bottom of the mine. The boys were stunned to see in the distance that the mine was filled with miners holding picks, shovels, and axes, working only by the light of oil lamps.

The brothers then saw an underground river running through the mine. The miners waded through the water, sifting wet sand through mesh screens, looking for pieces of gold.

"How can there still be miners here?" asked Rich.

"Look," said Jacob. "You can see right through them! It must be a special effect, like a **hologram**."

Before Rich could reply, their cart finally rolled to a stop. Stepping out, the brothers saw a bin filled with gold nuggets.

"Wow—look at all that gold!" Rich exclaimed.

"This gold has to be fake," said Jacob. "A **souvenir** for tourists. I guess we can take a few." Both boys started stuffing their pockets with the glittering nuggets.

"Thieves!" screamed one of the miners, pointing at the boys. "Here to steal our gold!"

"Well, we're not gonna let them!" shouted another. "Get 'em!"

The miners ran toward the boys with their picks, axes, and shovels raised like weapons.

"What do we do now?" cried Rich.

"Run!" shouted Jacob.

CHAPTER 4

Run for Your Life

Jacob and Rich ran, but the damp rocks on the floor of the mine were slippery. Rich slipped on a flat, wet rock and tumbled to the ground. Jacob skidded to a stop and turned back to help his brother up. The miners were getting closer.

The boys splashed across the river, soaking their sneakers. When they reached the other side, they saw a series of tunnels.

"In there!" shouted Jacob, pointing at the entrance to one of the tunnels.

"What?" cried Rich. "That dark tunnel?"

"No choice!" said Jacob.

A miner suddenly appeared in front of them, blocking their way into the tunnel.

"Nobody comes into our mine and steals our gold!" the miner shouted, raising his clenched fist in the air.

Jacob grabbed Rich's hand and they raced as fast as they could to get away from the angry miner. Jacob peered over his shoulder to see if the miner was chasing them, but he'd disappeared into thin air.

The oil lamps along the wall gave off just enough light for the boys to follow a narrow twisting path. Peering ahead, Rich saw a group of miners approaching, carrying flaming **flares** to light their way.

"Let's go here," Jacob whispered, turning into an even narrower passageway.

The boys moved quickly. A few seconds later, light glowed ahead of them. As the boys got closer to the light, they saw that it was coming from the flares held by the miners, who were now coming toward them. The boys wondered, *How had the miners gotten ahead of us? Just a minute ago, they were behind us.*

"What do we do?" cried Rich.

Jacob looked around and spotted a thin **crevice** in the rock wall. A pale light was shining through it.

"In here," he said to Rich. "It looks like we can just squeeze through. Come on."

The opening was so small the boys had to turn sideways to get in. **Shuffling** along with their hands touching the wall just a few inches in front of their faces, they snaked through the crevice.

A light grew brighter the further along they went.

"You won't get away, thieves!" the boys heard one of the miners shout.

A few minutes later, the narrow crevice opened up into a huge **cavern**. Stepping into the space, the boys saw the handcart that had brought them into the mine.

"We've gone in a complete circle!" said Rich.

"We have to get back in the cart," said Jacob. "It's the only way we'll get out of here. Let's make a run for it!"

Jacob and Rich dashed toward the handcart. Miners appeared out of nowhere and rushed toward them.

"We'll never make it!" cried Rich. "There are too many of them between us and the cart!"

Miners charged at the boys from every direction. The brothers ran but were quickly trapped with their backs against a wall. More and more miners started appearing out of thin air, as if every miner who had ever worked in the mine was coming back to get them.

"Gold thieves don't get out of this place alive!" snarled one of the miners.

Rich started to tremble.

Jacob looked all around, **desperately** searching for a way out. He spotted a wooden crate of flares. Next to the crate sat a pile of matches.

"Get ready to run, Rich," said Jacob as the miners moved **menacingly** closer.

Jacob grabbed a match and struck it against the wall. Its tip burst into flame. Jacob tossed the lit match into the crate. A few seconds later, the flares exploded in a burst of sparks and smoke.

The **billowing** smoke filled the mine.

"Now!" shouted Jacob. "Run!"

Hidden from the miners by the smoke, the boys raced back to the cart and started pumping their way out of the mine. A few minutes later, they were relieved to see sunlight pouring in through the mine's entrance. Then they hopped out of the cart and started running.

Soon, the boys reached Main Street, and the doors to every store suddenly burst open. Miners raced out onto the street, with their tools raised **threateningly** in the air. They surrounded Jacob and Rich. The shimmering, transparent ghosts were harder to see in the bright sunlight, but they were still terrifying.

"We know you took our gold," said a miner. "Give it back—all of it—right now!"

"Here," Rich said, pulling nuggets from his pockets. "We're sorry! We didn't know it was *real* gold."

Jacob reached into his right pocket and pulled out a handful of gold, tossing it at the miners. A shower of glittering nuggets rained down on the men, who dove toward the gold, climbing over each other.

"Run!" shouted Rich. As the miners fought over the gold, Jacob and Rich ran down the street.

27

Moments later, Jacob and Rich arrived at the Hardstone sign at the town entrance. Both of their parents were there waiting for them. The boys were out of breath and relieved to be safe.

"Where have you been?" yelled Dad. "I woke up and you were gone. I looked everywhere for you two!"

"Oh, honey, they're safe. They were just off exploring," Mom said calmly, adding, "Boys, I got you a book about the town of Hardstone. According to this book, the miners in the town never left. They refused to leave their **claims**—even after they died—for fear that someone else would come along and steal their gold. And now, if anyone sets foot in the town to try and take their gold, the ghosts will chase them out. Anyway, I thought you'd enjoy this. Of course, ghost stories aren't true."

Jacob leaned over to his brother. "I'm glad we left all the gold we took back in town," he whispered. "I'd hate to have those miners keep chasing us."

Rich slipped his hand into his left pocket and felt the one gold nugget he had kept. He glanced anxiously over his shoulder—would the miners *really* keep chasing them? At that moment, the wind began to blow again. And Rich thought he could hear a strained voice, but he wasn't quite able to make out what it was saying.

Terror at the Ghost Town Mine

1. Jacob and Rich learn about the Gold Rush at the Miner's Museum. What was the Gold Rush and when did it occur? Use examples from the story to explain.

2. Hardstone is called a ghost town by the guard at the museum. What is a ghost town?

3. What is happening in this scene (top picture)?

4. Where are Jacob and Rich going in the handcart (bottom picture)?

5. In the story, the boys explore a real ghost town. Would you like to visit a ghost town? Explain why you would or wouldn't want to.

GLOSSARY

abandoned (uh-BAN-duhnd) no longer in use

barren (BAR-uhn) unable to produce crops

billowing (BIL-oh-ing) rising up, or rolling like waves

bolts (BOHLTS) rolls of something, such as cloth

cavern (KAV-urn) a room in a cave

claims (KLAYMZ) land for mining

crevice (KREV-iss) a narrow opening

desperately (DEHS-pur-it-*lee*) done with an urgent need

flares (FLAIRZ) torches that burn to create bright light

frigid (FRIJ-id) extremely cold

hologram (HAH-luh-gram) an image made by laser light beams

menacingly (MEN-is-ing-lee) dangerously, causing fear

reluctantly (ri-LUHK-tuhnt-*lee*) with hesitation or unwillingness

rigged (RIGD) arranged in a dishonest way

shards (SHAHRDZ) broken pieces

shuffling (SHUHF-uhl-ing) walking slowly, dragging one's feet along the ground or floor

sifting (SIFT-ing) separating large and small pieces using a mesh or sieve

souvenir (soo-vuh-NEER) an object you keep that reminds you of a place, person, or event

strained (STRAYND) tense or stressed

threateningly (THREH-tin-ing-*lee*) in a harmful manner

trudged (TRUHJD) walked slowly, dragging one's feet

tumbleweed (TUM-buhl-*weed*) a broken-off piece of a plant that blows around in the wind

ABOUT THE AUTHOR

Michael Teitelbaum is the author of more than 150 children's books, including young adult and middle-grade novels, tie-in novelizations, and picture books. His most recent books are *The Very Hungry Zombie: A Parody* and its sequel *The Very Thirsty Vampire: A Parody*, both created with illustrator Jon Apple. Michael and his wife, Sheleigah, live with two talkative cats in a farmhouse (as yet unhaunted) in upstate New York.

ABOUT THE ILLUSTRATORS

Olga and Aleksey Ivanov are a family team of children's book illustrators, and they have illustrated more than 70 books. Their most recent project was a "Lassie Come Home" picture book. Olga and Aleksey live and work in their mountain home/studio with a couple of Samoyed dogs in gorgeous Evergreen, Colorado.